VANILLA ICE CREAM

*For Vivian,
and for sparrows*

VANILLA
ICE CREAM

Bob Graham

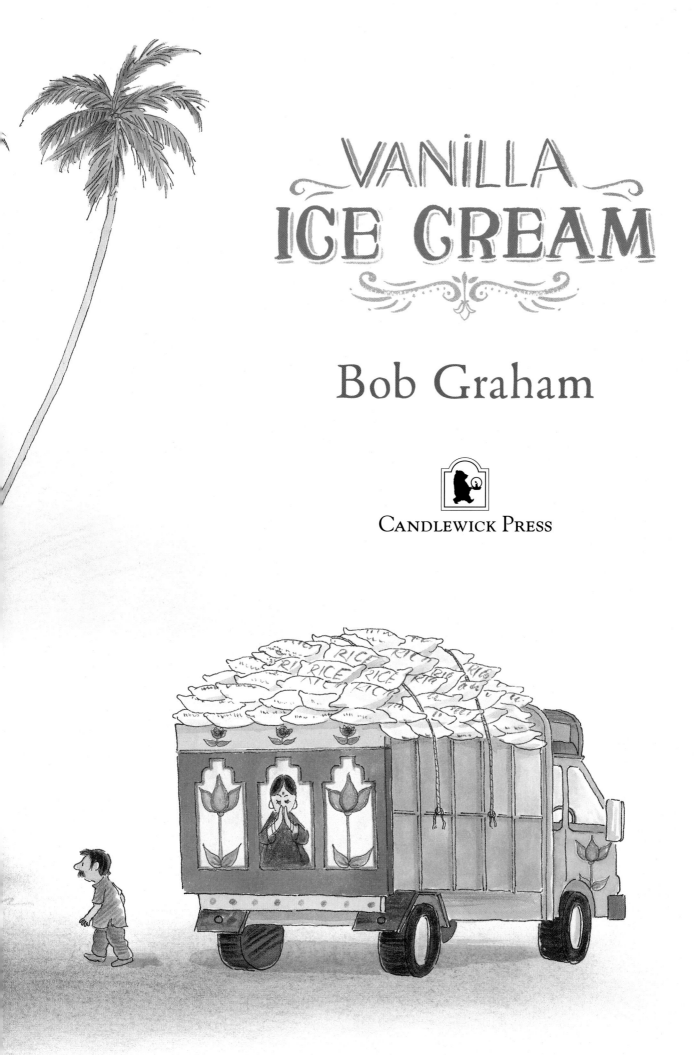

CANDLEWICK PRESS

The young sparrow rises from the dust.
He looks down at Annisha and Suhani.

He is young. He is curious . . .

and bold.

Bold as a
truck-stop sparrow.

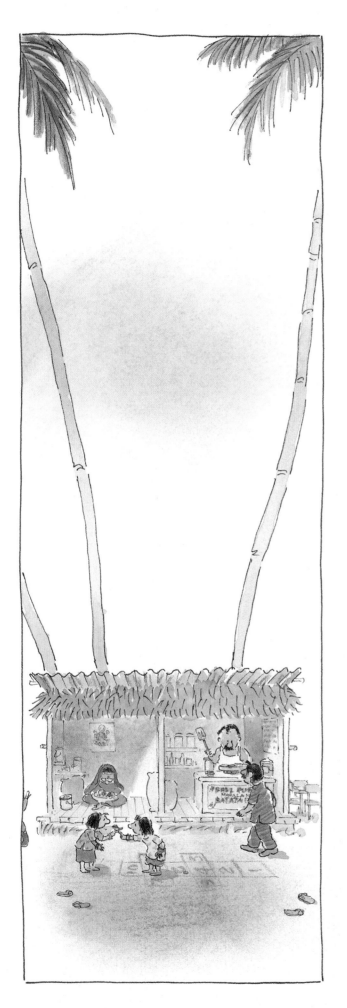

The sparrow is free to go where he pleases.

And to eat . . .

what he can find.

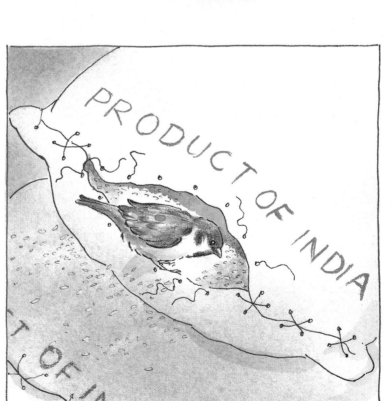

While the other birds
scuffle in the dust . . .

the sparrow leaves the truck stop forever.

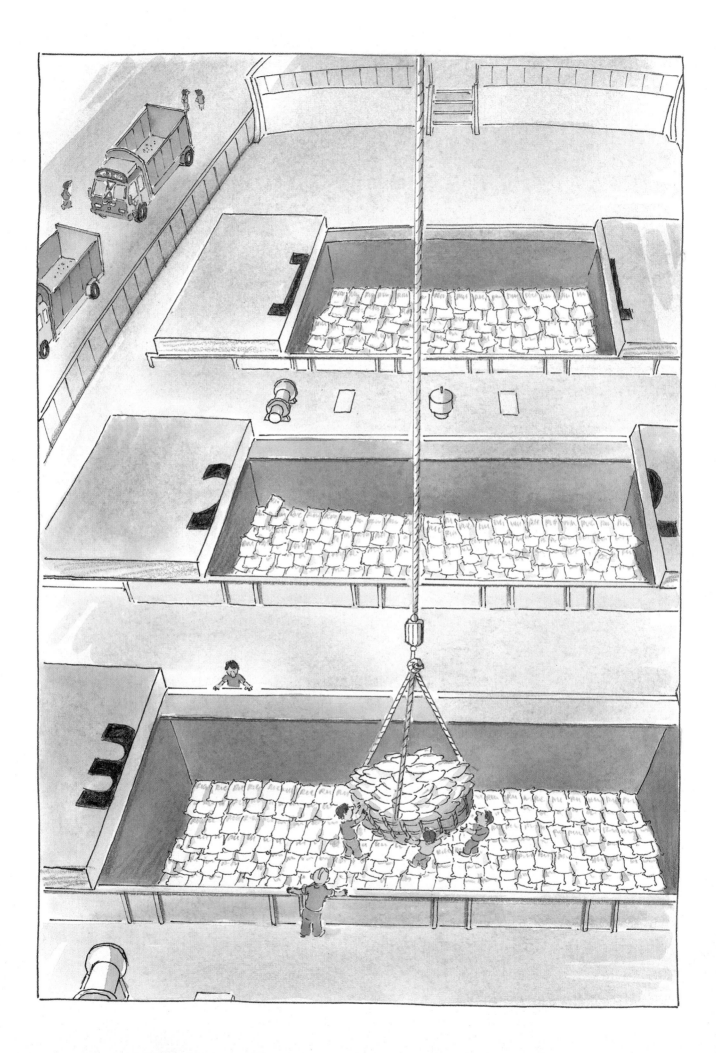

Like all wild birds, he follows the food.

The truck-stop sparrow heads south.

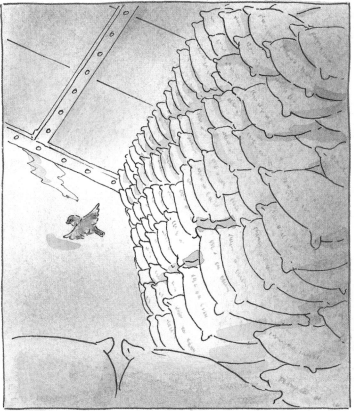

He arrives into a bright new day.

Somewhere, somehow, in this vast city he finds . . .

Edie Irvine . . .

and her grandma and granddad.

So it is . . .

at the Café Botanica . . .

in just one fleeting moment . . .

Edie's life changes forever.

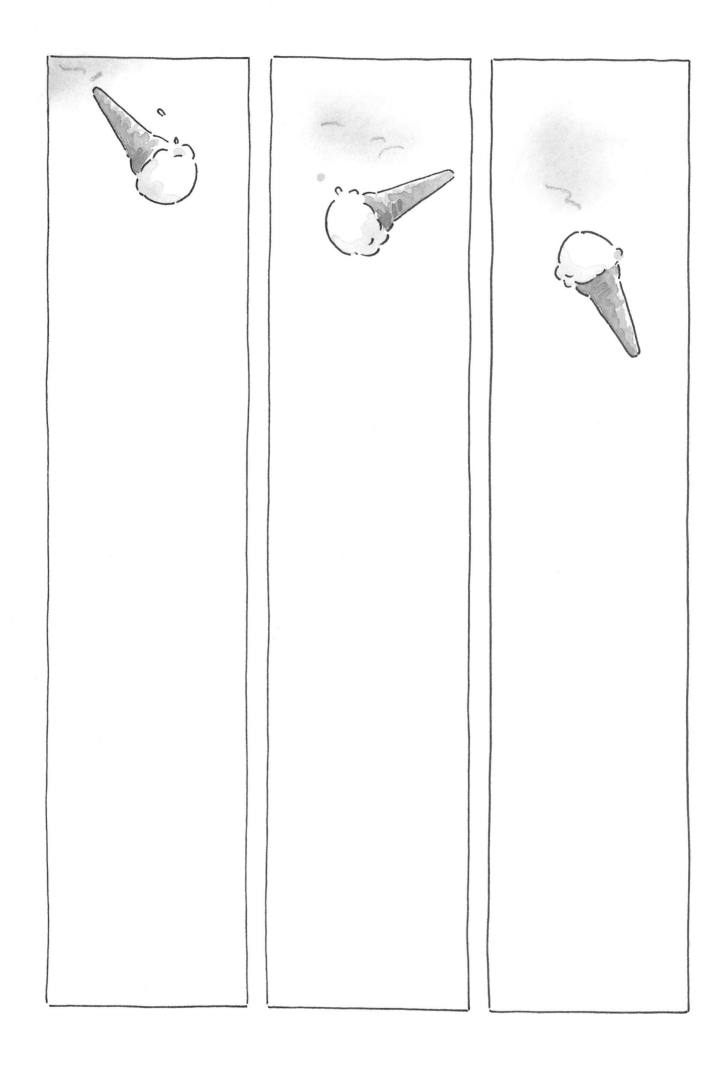

Edie Irvine, also young and curious,
for the very first time . . .

discovers the taste of vanilla ice cream.

First U.S. edition 2014. Library of Congress Catalog Card Number 2013952841. ISBN 978-0-7636-7377-2. This book was typeset in Poliphilus. The illustrations were done in ink and watercolor. Candlewick Press, 99 Dover Street, Somerville, Massachusetts 02144. visit us at www.candlewick.com. Printed in Shenzhen, Guangdong, China. 14 15 16 17 18 19 CCP 10 9 8 7 6 5 4 3 2 1